THE CAT'S PAJAMAS

WRITTEN and ILLUSTRATED
by DANIEL WALLACE

INKSHARES
CROWDFUNDED PUBLISHING

Copyright © 2014 by Daniel Wallace

Written and illustrated by Daniel Wallace
Edited by Kim Keller
Designed by Rob Cameron

Published by Inkshares, Inc.
San Francisco, California

Printed in China

First edition
Printed in 2014

2 3 4 5 6 7 8 9 10

Library of Congress Cataloging-in-Publication Data is available.

ISBN 978-1-941758-00-7
(hardcover)

For Frances, a very cool cat

LONG, LONG AGO, WHEN CATS looked alike, talked alike, and, most importantly, *dressed* alike, there was Louis Fellini. He was a different sort of cat.

There was a time when cats lived in houses and went to school and had to go to work in a city full of cats. All the father cats wore the same suits and ties, and mother cats wore the same kinds of dresses. Teeny-tiny kittens wore itty-bitty kitty underpants, and the cats who were boys and girls wore the same socks and shoes and T-shirts and shorts. Why? Because that's how it had been since anyone could remember.

No one had that special something, that crazy spark, that who-cares-what-the-other-cats-think drive for something new, something different, something all your own and nobody else's. It's always like this until somebody comes along to shake things up.

In this story, that somebody is Louis.

"Can't somebody around here be a little *different*?" he yowled from time to time.

Well, Louis could.

When he was a kitten, he didn't wear the itty-bitty kitty underpants all his kitten friends did. Louis insisted on wearing a grass skirt for pants and a paper bag for a shirt, which nobody *ever* wore.

This embarrassed his parents so
much they almost never let him outside
when there were other cats around,
which meant they could *never* go on
picnics (cats used to *love* to go on picnics).
But that was okay with Louis.

But when he started going to school, there was not much his parents could do. His mother and father both worked and had to leave the house early.

Louis dressed himself. So when every other cat in his whole school came dressed in shorts and a T-shirt, Louis wore a little French beret and a cape and stars on his shoes. He didn't mind it when every single cat in school stared at him as though he were crazy, because that's what happens when you're a little different. Sometimes you get stared at.

Anyway, he liked his cape and beret. He looked *good*, if he did say so himself.

    He looked so good, he wore it to school everyday that week. And then a funny thing happened.

    The next week, every cat—and this was a lot of cats, a very large number of cats—came to school wearing a cape and beret, nearly identical to the cape and beret Louis wore! And they *all* had *stars* on their shoes!

"What's going on?" he said to a group of cats leaning against the school wall, just leaning there, feeling pretty cool in their capes and berets with stars on their shoes.

"It's time cats wore a different kind of thing," one of the cats told him. "That T-shirt and shorts outfit was getting pretty old. It's the sort of thing our parents might wear, you know?"

Louis knew only too well.

"So it came to us, sort of all at once: *Let's do something new.* Let's be ourselves, in a way which, being ourselves, only we can be. So we came up with this. The stars, the cape, the beret. Much like you," he said.

"You mean *exactly* like me," Louis said.

Louis shook his head and sighed.

"But the new look," he said, "was *my* look. At least, that's what I thought."

"Apparently not," the cat said. "I mean, look around you. Everybody's wearing the exact same thing."

"It's a wonderfully new, wonderfully different kind of thing."

And yet, Louis thought, not so wonderful, new and different as when he had been the only one doing it.

So the next week, Louis changed. He was still different, but now he was a different sort of different.

He wore sunglasses, a purple plastic jacket, and green boots that came up to his knees almost. Once again, he was different from everybody else, and once again, this time the very next day, all the other cats came to school dressed *exactly* the same way Louis dressed, right down to the clothespin he had hanging from his tail.

"As you can see," a cat said to Louis, "the new look suddenly became old. So here we are with this new look and we feel pretty good about it."

"I felt pretty good about it, too…" Louis said. "Yesterday."

"That was then, this is now," the cat said. "Times change. Cats have to change with them. What's the problem?"

Poor Louis was about to go completely crazy.

"The problem?" he said. "THE PROBLEM? You're all just a bunch of COPY CATS, that's the problem."

That night, after slipping into his wonderfully comfortable pajamas, Louis couldn't sleep. *He* had a problem now. All he wanted to be was himself. Inside, he knew he was different, and he thought that was probably true for the other cats, too. Louis only knew one way to show his difference: his clothes.

So that night he stayed up very late thinking about what he could wear to school tomorrow, thinking and thinking as the hours ticked away, and in the morning he slept through his alarm. He ran off to catch the bus in a rush, without even eating his breakfast, without even a sip of milk.

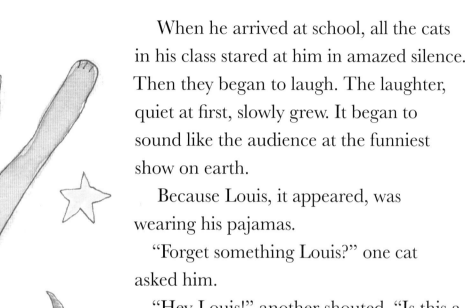

When he arrived at school, all the cats in his class stared at him in amazed silence. Then they began to laugh. The laughter, quiet at first, slowly grew. It began to sound like the audience at the funniest show on earth.

Because Louis, it appeared, was wearing his pajamas.

"Forget something Louis?" one cat asked him.

"Hey Louis!" another shouted. "Is this a dream? Are you sleepwalking? You forgot to get dressed!"

The truth is, he *had* forgotten to get dressed. But there was something so wonderfully new and different about it, something so edgy and bright and fine, something, in short, so *him*—that he yawned in a happy way, the happiest way a cat can yawn, and said, "Me? Forget to dress? You've got to be kidding."

Of course, I would like to tell you now that none of the other cats could go quite this far—I mean, pajamas, for goodness sake!—and that Louis was the only cat in the history of cats to ever wear his pajamas to school. But they could go that far. They could and they did.

The very next day, all his cat friends came to school yawning and wearing their pajamas and leaning against the school wall. Of course they did. It was cool and different and most of all, it was comfortable. It was so clearly comfortable, so clearly fine and wonderful, that after a while even the *teachers* came to school wearing their pajamas.

Newspaper articles were written about it, and this new style of cat clothes became the most talked about thing on television. The cats who made cat pajamas became overrun with orders, and so they began to make more of them, more and more, and they made them more wonderful than ever—so wonderful that everybody, *everybody*, found that removing them in the morning became a real chore.

No one wanted to get out of something so comfortable. Pajamas were so soft and warm and easy to nap in. Wearing suits and ties felt like wearing steel wool and cardboard. Even T-shirts and shorts were too scritchy and scratchy! Pajamas were perfect. Cats started sleeping . . . a lot. And even the cats who woke up and went to work and school didn't get much done. All they could think about were pajamas.

Eventually, cats everywhere simply stayed at home in their pajamas, and they were happy doing it. But their whole world began to change and, eventually, just…fall apart. With no cats going to work, the houses, office buildings, and restaurants crumbled into dust, and finally the pajama makers and then the pajamas themselves disappeared.

And that's when cats as they *were* became cats as they *are*, and by the time people – you and me and the others like us – came around, which wasn't for many, many years, they thought cats had always been furry, purring, fun-loving creatures, who liked nothing better than to knock a crumpled up piece of paper around with their paws, or find a warm spot somewhere to curl up, yawn, and sleep.

But the truth is, they haven't always been like that. They used to be different.

And to think it all started with just one cat, trying as hard as he could to be himself, and sleeping late in the morning because of it.

But Louis was happy. Because he realized that it's not so much about *being* different as it is about *making* a difference. And that's exactly what Louis did.

GRAND PATRONS

The Cat's Pajamas *was made possible by crowdfunding on inkshares.com.*
Special thanks to the following cool cats:

Alec T. Coquin • Ann Stewart • Anna Barker • Barnaby Conrad III
Carol G. Rosen • Cheri Bowers • Christopher Kubica • Daniel Cross Turner
Daniel Kellison • Druscilla French • Elisabeth Benfey • Elizabeth Woodman
Hannah Butensky • Flyleaf Books • Jane Holding • Jay Miller
Jeffrey A. Polish • John August • Katherine Sandoz • Keebe Fitch
Kevin Budner • Laura Frankstone • Lois Watts • Margaret D. Whiteside
Margaret W. Rich • Marianne Levitsky • Mark E. Madsen • Michael Malone
Nancy C. Demorest • Pamela A. Mann • Radu Mihaescu • Rangeley Wallace
Richard Green • Rob Chappelhow • Roger C. Kellison • Sarah W. Whiteside
Spencer Woodman • Steve Mack • The Tuesday Agency • Yasmin Harrison